Ladybird Readers

Black Beauty

Series Editor: Sorrel Pitts
Text adapted by Sorrel Pitts
Illustrated by Kasia Matyjaszek

LADYBIRD BOOKS

UK | USA | Canada | Ireland | Australia
India | New Zealand | South Africa

Ladybird Books is part of the Penguin Random House group of companies
whose addresses can be found at global.penguinrandomhouse.com.
www.penguin.co.uk   www.puffin.co.uk   www.ladybird.co.uk

First published 2018
002

Copyright © Ladybird Books Ltd, 2018

Printed in China

A CIP catalogue record for this book is available from the British Library

ISBN: 978–0–241–33617–5

All correspondence to
Ladybird Books
Penguin Random House Children's
80 Strand, London WC2R 0RL

MIX
Paper from
responsible sources
FSC® C018179

Black Beauty

Characters

Black Beauty

Ginger

Mr. Gordon

James Howard

Joe Green

Alfred Smirk

Reuben Smith

Chapter One
My First Years

I was born in a beautiful field. There were other foals there. I played with them, but sometimes they kicked me and bit me.

One day my mother said to me, "These **foals*** don't have **good manners**. I want you to be a **gentle** horse with good manners. You must never bite or kick."

I grew up to be a handsome horse. I was black, with one white foot and a white star on my face.

When I was four, my **master** put a **saddle** on my back, and then he rode me. After that, metal shoes were put on my feet. They felt **stiff** and heavy at first.

*Definitions of words in **bold** can be found in the glossary on pages 55–56

Next, my master taught me to pull a **cart** and a **carriage**. When he was riding me, he taught me to go slow when he pulled the **reins**, or to go fast if he pressed the saddle with his legs.

Now that I was ready to be sold, my mother came and spoke to me. "I hope a good man will buy you," she said, "but a horse never knows."

CHAPTER TWO

At Mr. Gordon's Farm

In May, I was sold to Mr. Gordon. I was put in a big **stable** with four stalls. Our **groom** was called James Howard. In the next **stall** there was a horse called Merrylegs, who Mr. Gordon's children rode.

The next day, my new master rode me for the first time. He was very pleased with me.

"What shall we call him?" Mr. Gordon said to his wife.

"He has a very handsome face," she replied. "How about Black Beauty?"

There was another horse in the stable called Ginger, who told me about her life before she was bought by Mr. Gordon.

"My first **owners** made me wear a **bearing rein** which made my neck very stiff," she said. "I became angry and jumped and kicked—so they sold me. It's better here, of course, but that might change."

Luckily, Ginger was wrong. Our new owner, Mr. Gordon, was kind, and he never made us wear a bearing rein.

Chapter Three
The Bridge

One day in the autumn, my master and James had to go on a long journey. I pulled a small cart, and we went along the road until we came to a bridge. The bridge was flat, and because the water in the river was quite high, it nearly reached it.

We returned home late that evening. It was very windy—a storm was coming, and it was nearly dark when we reached the bridge again. I could see that the water was now covering the middle of the bridge. Suddenly, I felt strange, so I stopped.

"Go on, Beauty," said Mr. Gordon, but I would not move.

At that moment, we heard a voice shout, "Stop! Don't cross!"

It was a man from the village. "The bridge is broken," he shouted. "You can't cross it."

"Thank you, Beauty!" said my master.

That night I was given a warm dinner, and a thick bed of **straw**. This made me happy, because I was very tired.

CHAPTER FOUR
A Fire!

My master and **mistress** decided to visit some friends who lived about fifty miles away. It was a long journey, but James drove Ginger and me carefully, and as evening came, we arrived at the town where the friends lived.

Ginger and I were taken to a rented stable where many other horses were staying.

I was very tired and quickly went to sleep. When I woke up, my nose was full of smoke, and I couldn't breathe. There was a strange noise, which frightened me.

The groom, Dick Towler, tried to pull the horses from their stalls, but we were all too afraid to move.

Then, James came in and spoke to me in a gentle voice. "Come with me, Beauty," he said. He tied his scarf over my eyes. I let him lead me out of the stable, because I trusted him.

A man took me, and James went back to get Ginger.

Chapter Five

James Says Goodbye

One by one, the horses slowly came out of the stalls. The fire engine came soon after, and the fire was stopped. No horses died, but some of them were hurt.

Later, we learned that Dick Towler was smoking a **pipe** when the fire started. After that, pipes were never allowed in Mr. Gordon's stable again.

Ginger and I were glad to get home, but the next day we heard some bad news.

James was going to leave us.

19

A new groom called Joe Green came to take his job. At first we weren't sure about Joe, but he was gentle and kind, and we soon started to like him.

Finally, the morning came when James had to leave. We were all very sad as we watched him walk out of the gate.

CHAPTER SIX

Our Mistress is Ill

Soon after James left, I was woken in the night by Joe. "Wake up, Beauty," he said. "We must ride fast now. Our mistress is ill, and she needs the doctor."

We rode fast over the hills, and arrived at the doctor's house at 3 a.m.

"My mistress is ill, sir," said Joe. "You must come immediately!"

"I can't," replied the doctor. "My horse has been out all day, and it's tired.

"You can borrow my horse," said Joe.

So, the doctor made me run very fast all the way back to Mr. Gordon's house. When I was put back in my stall, my legs were shaking.

After that, I became very ill, and everyone thought I was going to die.

When I finally got better, I heard that sad things were going to happen. Our mistress had to move to a warm country because she was ill, and the horses were going to be sold.

At last, the day came when we took her to the train station. "We will never see her again," said Joe, sadly.

Chapter Seven
At Earlshall Park

The next morning, Joe took Merrylegs to a neighbor, who wanted him for his children. Then, Ginger and I were taken to Earlshall Park, our new home.

"We have never used a bearing rein with these horses," Joe explained to our new master.

"Well, they will have to use one here," he replied.

The next day, I had to wear a bearing rein for the first time. It was very **uncomfortable**, and it was difficult to pull the cart up hills.

I was unhappy, and Ginger hated it. She kicked so much that she fell down on the road. After that, she was used for **hunting**, and I was given a new partner called Max.

Although I was fed good food, and my stable was clean, I did not feel I had any friends at Earlshall Park and the bearing rein was always tight and uncomfortable. I became unhappy, because I was lonely and I hated my work.

Chapter Eight

A Fall on the Road

When my master and mistress went to London for the spring, a groom called Reuben Smith managed the horses. Smith was a good man, but sometimes he rode us too fast.

One evening, Reuben Smith rode me into town. He was late finishing his business, and it was dark when he came to fetch me.

He rode me back in a hurry, and didn't notice that one of my shoes was falling off. Then, he hit me, and I ran faster. The shoe suddenly came off, and I fell on to my knees. Reuben Smith was thrown on to the road.

I heard him breathing for a while, and then it stopped . . .

He was dead.

I was put in a field for my knees to get better. Ginger was there, too. She also needed to rest, because the hunting was hard, and she was tired.

One day my master came to see me. "We cannot have that horse pulling the cart," he said. "His knees are too bad. We will have to sell him."

Chapter Nine

Life as a Job Horse

A week later, I was sold to some stables to work as a "job horse"—this meant I could be rented to carriage drivers, or to anyone who needed a horse.

I was quiet and gentle, so I was often rented to the worst drivers, because I never kicked or bit them.

One day, a man called Mr. Barry came and took me out. He was a good and gentle driver, and when we returned he decided that he wanted to buy me.

At first this was good. My groom, a man called Mr. Filcher, looked after me well, and kept my stable clean.

After a few weeks, I noticed that I was getting less food, and then *no* food. I soon became weak.

A friend of Mr. Barry's noticed how thin I was. "Is your horse eating the oats that you buy for him?" he asked.

Mr. Barry was surprised. He discovered that Mr. Filcher's wife was giving my food to their rabbits, which they sold at the market!

Chapter Ten

A Lazy Groom

Mr. Filcher was sent to prison for two months, and Mr. Barry had to employ a new groom. His name was Alfred Smirk, and he was very handsome—but he loved himself too much!

Mr. Smirk was never cruel to me, but he was lazy. He never brushed me, and he never cleaned my feet.

He also didn't clean my stable enough, and my feet soon hurt from standing on wet, dirty straw all the time.

When I nearly fell twice in one afternoon, Mr. Barry called the vet.

"Your horse's feet are hurting him because his straw is dirty," the vet said.

Then, he cleaned my feet, and he told Alfred to change my straw and clean the floor.

I was soon better, but Mr. Barry was so angry because of both his grooms' lies that he decided to sell all his horses.

So, I had to be sold again.

CHAPTER ELEVEN
My Final Home

While I was waiting at the horse sale,
a farmer came up to me, and he felt my
shoulder with his hand.

"This is a good horse, Willie," he said
to a young boy at his side, "but he's not
been lucky."

"Poor boy," said Willie. "Can you buy him
and make him strong again, Grandfather?"

The farmer walked me up and down.
"He'll be a good horse again," he said.
"I'll buy him."

After that, I had good food, and I was
looked after well. One day, the farmer's
wife came to ride me.

"I like him," she said. "Please can I try him for a few weeks?"

The next day, I was taken to a comfortable stable. As the groom was cleaning my face, he said, "That is like Black Beauty's star! Is this him?"

The groom was Joe Green!

My troubles are finished now. I've lived here for many years, and I'll never be sold.

I am very happy here, but sometimes I still like to dream I'm with my old friends, Merrylegs and Ginger, standing quietly together under the apple tree at Mr. Gordon's farm.

The activities at the back of this book help you to practice the following skills:

- Spelling and writing

- Reading

- Speaking

- Listening

- Critical thinking

- Preparation for the Cambridge Young Learners exams

1 **Choose the correct words, and write the full sentences in your notebook.** 📖 ✏️

1 Black Beauty was born in a beautiful **home. / field.**

2 His mother wanted him to be **gentle. / handsome.**

3 Black Beauty was black, with one **white / brown** foot.

4 At the age of four, Black Beauty's master **road / rode** him.

2 **Read the answers, and write the questions in your notebook.** 📖 ✏️

1 They felt stiff and heavy.

2 He pulled the reins.

3 He pressed the saddle with his legs.

4 Because he was ready to be sold.

3 Complete the sentences using words from Chapter Two. Write the full sentences in your notebook. 📖 ✏️ ⭐

1 Black Beauty was sold . . .

2 In the stall next to Black Beauty . . .

3 A horse called Ginger told Black Beauty about . . .

4 Their new owner, Mr. Gordon, was . . .

4 Read the definitions. Write the correct words in your notebook. 📖 ✏️

1 a building where people keep horses   **s** . . .

2 a person who owns something   **o** . . .

3 a seat that is put on a horse for a person to ride it   **s** . . .

4 a person whose job it is to feed and care for horses   **g** . . .

5 a part of a stable, big enough for one animal to live in   **s** . . .

6 difficult to move   **s** . . .

5 Listen to Chapter Three. Answer the questions in your notebook. *✏

1 Who did Black Beauty take on a long journey?

2 When did they return home?

3 What could Black Beauty see in the middle of the bridge?

4 Why did Black Beauty stop?

5 What did the man from the village shout?

6 Talk to a friend about the characters below. 💬

Black Beauty is a handsome horse. He . . .

7 Choose the correct answers. Write the full sentences in your notebook. 📖 ✏️ 🔖

1 Who did Beauty's master and mistress visit?
   a James   **b** some friends
   c Ginger   **d** their children

2 What time of day did they arrive at the town?
   a evening   **b** morning
   c night   **d** lunchtime

3 What was in the stable when Beauty woke up?
   a water   **b** smoke
   c straw   **d** Mr. Gordon

4 What frightened Beauty?
   a the groom   **b** a woman
   c a horse   **d** a noise

5 Who spoke to Beauty in a gentle voice?
   a Dick Towler   **b** Mr. Gordon
   c James   **d** Mrs. Gordon

8 Write a news story about the fire in Chapter Four. Write it in your notebook. ✏️ ❓

FIRE IN STABLE

Last night, there was a large fire in a stable . . .

9 Ask and answer the questions with
a friend. Then, ask your own questions.

1 *What came to the stable to stop the fire?*

A fire engine.

2 Did any horses die in the fire?

3 How did the fire start?

4 What bad news did Ginger and Beauty hear?

10 Match the two parts of the sentences.
Write the full sentences in your notebook.

1 After the fire, pipes were

2 When Ginger and Beauty got home,

3 A new groom was coming

4 The new groom, Joe Green,

a they heard some bad news.

b was gentle and kind.

c never allowed in Mr. Gordon's stable again.

d to take James' job.

11 Are sentences 1—5 *True* or *False*?
If there is not enough information write,
Doesn't say. Write the answers in your
notebook. 📖 ✏️

1 James came to the stable and woke Beauty
up in the night.

2 Mrs. Gordon was ill and needed a doctor.

3 They rode for five hours to get to the doctor.

4 The doctor rode his horse back to
Mr. Gordon's house.

5 Mrs. Gordon had to move to a warm country.

12 You are Mrs. Gordon. Ask and answer the
questions with a friend, using the words
in the box. 💬

ill   Joe and Black Beauty   warm country   sell

1 *I don't feel very good. What is wrong with me?*

You are ill.

2 Who can get the doctor for me?

3 What will help me get better?

4 What will we do with the horses?

13 Choose the correct words, and write the full sentences in your notebook. 📖 ✏️ 🏵️

1	master.	groom.	home.
2	a saddle	a bearing rein	shoes
3	pulled a cart	fell down	ran fast
4	bad	very bad	good
5	kicked	hated	used

1 Earlshall Park was Ginger and Beauty's new . . .

2 At Earlshall Park, Beauty had to wear . . . for the first time.

3 After she . . . on the road, Ginger was used for hunting.

4 The food was . . . at Earlshall Park.

5 Beauty was lonely and he . . . his work.

14 Listen to Chapter Seven. Describe Beauty's life at Earlshall Park in your notebook. 🎧*✏️

Beauty's life at Earlshall Park . . .

15 Read the sentences. If a sentence is not correct, write the correct sentence in your notebook. 📖 ✏️

1 The groom, Reuben Smith, managed the horses for the winter.

2 One evening, Reuben Smith rode Ginger into town.

3 It was light when they rode back home.

4 Reuben Smith didn't notice that one of Beauty's shoes was falling off.

16 Look at the picture and read the questions. Write the answers in your notebook. 📖 ✏️ ✿

1 Who was riding Beauty home in a hurry?

2 What was the problem with Beauty's feet?

3 What did the man who is riding Beauty do to him?

4 What happened when Beauty fell on to his knees?

17 Read the questions. Write full sentences in your notebook using the words in the box. 📖 ✒️

> less food   rent(ed)   at first   buy
> carriage drivers   well   clean   weak

1 What did a "job horse" do?

2 What did Mr. Barry decide to do?

3 How did Mr. Filcher look after Beauty at first?

4 What happened after a few weeks?

18 Read the text, then write all the text with the correct verbs in your notebook. 📖 ✒️

After a few weeks, Beauty . . . (**notice**) that he was getting less food. Then, he was getting *no* food and he soon . . . (**become**) weak. Mr. Barry was surprised that Beauty . . . (**be**) so thin. Then, Mr. Barry . . . (**discover**) that Mr. Filcher's wife . . . (**take**) Beauty's food. Mrs. Filcher . . . (**give**) the food to her rabbits, and then . . . (**sell**) them at the market.

19 Read the text below. Find the five mistakes, and write the correct sentences in your notebook. 📖 ✏️

Mr. Filcher was sent to prison for two years. Now, Beauty had another new groom. His name was Alfred Smirk.

Mr. Smirk never cleaned Beauty's feet, or his stable. After some time, Beauty's feet hurt and Mr. Barry called the doctor. Beauty's feet were hurting because his straw was dirty. Mr. Barry cleaned Beauty's feet, and told his wife to change his straw.

Beauty got better, but Mr. Barry was angry with the grooms and decided to sell all his stables.

20 Write some instructions in your notebook to help Alfred Smirk look after Black Beauty well. ✏️ ❓

1. You must brush Black Beauty every day.

21 **Write the answers to the questions in your notebook.**

1 Who came up to Beauty at the horse sale?

2 What did Willie want his grandfather to do?

3 What did Willie's grandfather do?

4 Who wanted to try Beauty for a few weeks?

5 Who was the groom at Beauty's new stable?

6 Does Beauty have a good life now?

22 **Talk to a friend about Black Beauty's life. Ask and answer questions.**

1

> Where was Beauty born?

> He was born in a beautiful field.

2 How many different stables did Beauty live at?

3 What were the names of Beauty's owners?

4 Is Beauty's life happy or sad?

5 Who were the good people in Beauty's life?

23 Look online or in a library, and find out five interesting things about horses.

Talk to a friend. Say something about horses that is true, and something that is not true.

Ask your friend to guess which thing is true.

Then, listen to your friend, and guess which of the things they say is true.

24 Anna Sewell wrote *Black Beauty* in 1877. Look online, or in the library, and answer the questions below in your notebook.

- Where was Anna Sewell born?

- Did she write any other books?

- When did she die?

- Are there any famous films of *Black Beauty*?

- Which character would you most like to be in the book, and why?

Now, make a poster about Anna Sewell. Work in a group, and show your work.

Write a review of this book in your notebook. Did you like it? Why? / Why not?

In your review, include the following information:

- which character you like the most

- what part of the story you like the most

- which picture you like the most

Glossary

bearing rein *(noun)*
this goes under a horse's neck, to make it lift its head up

carriage *(noun)*
a large box with wheels that people sit in, and that is pulled by a horse

cart *(noun)*
a box with wheels used to hold things, that is pulled by a horse

foal *(noun)*
a very young horse

gentle *(adjective)*
If you are kind, calm, quiet and careful, you are *gentle*.

good manners *(noun)*
If you have *good manners*, you act in a way that is kind.

groom *(noun)*
a person whose job is to feed and care for horses

hunting *(noun)*
a sport where people on horses follow animals and kill them

master *(noun)*
a man who has people working for him

mistress *(noun)*
a woman who has people working for her

owner *(noun)*
a person who owns something

pipe *(noun)*
a long piece of wood that people use to smoke

reins *(noun)*
These go around a horse and are used to control the direction it moves in.

saddle *(noun)*
a seat that is put on a horse for a person to ride it

stable *(noun)*
a building where people keep horses

stall *(noun)*
a part of a stable, big enough for one animal to live in

stiff *(adjective)*
difficult to move

straw *(noun)*
Grass and parts of other plants that are very dry. Some farm animals eat straw, and sleep on it.

uncomfortable *(adjective)*
If something doesn't feel good to wear, sit on, sleep on, etc., it is *uncomfortable*.